Big Bear
Little Bear

For Deborah
~ *DB*

For Noah who is little, and
for Jake who wants to be BIG
~ *JC*

ISBN 0-439-31884-X

12 11 10 9 8 7 6 5 4 3 2 1   2 3 4 5 6 7/0

Printed in the U.S.A.   24

First Scholastic printing, January 2002

Big Bear
Little Bear

DAVID BEDFORD AND JANE CHAPMAN

SCHOLASTIC INC.

New York   Toronto   London   Auckland   Sydney
Mexico City   New Delhi   Hong Kong   Buenos Aires

One bright and cold morning,
Little Bear helped Mama Bear
scoop snow out of their den.

"This will make more room for you to play,"
said Mama Bear. "You are getting bigger."

"I am?" asked Little Bear.
"What is it like to be big?"

"When you are big, you can roll
little bears in the soft snow,"
said Mother Bear.

Little Bear giggled as he
turned over and over.

"When I am big, will I run as fast as you?" Little Bear asked as he hurried to keep up with Mama Bear.

"Oh yes," said Mama Bear,
and she waited for Little Bear
to catch up with her.

Mama Bear helped
Little Bear climb
onto her shoulders.
"I'll show you
what it is like
to be grown-up",
she said.

"I can see to the
end of the world,"
cried Little Bear.
He reached up.
"And I can almost
touch the sky!"

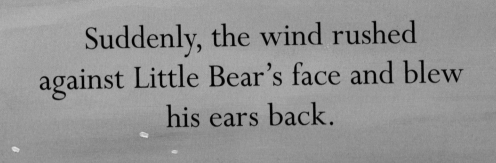

Suddenly, the wind rushed
against Little Bear's face and blew
his ears back.

"Hold on tight!" cried Mama Bear. "Is this how I'll run when I am grown-up?" wondered Little Bear.

"I am flying like a bird!"
shouted Little Bear.

"Hold your breath!"
Mama Bear called.

SPLASH!

"When I am big, I will dive into the water and swim like a fish," Little Bear thought to himself. He watched his mother carefully so he would know how.

Mama Bear climbed out of the water with Little Bear clinging tightly to her back.

"When I am big I want to do everything grown-ups can," said Little Bear.

"You will," said Mama Bear
as she carried Little Bear
back to their snow den.

"Will I feel as if I can touch
the sky and run as fast
as the wind and
swim like a fish?"
asked Little Bear.
"Yes," said Mama Bear.
"That is what happens
when little bears grow big."

Suddenly, Little Bear yawned.
It had been a busy day.
"I am going to like being grown-up one day,"
said Little Bear sleepily . . .

"especially when
you'll be there
to show me how."
He snuggled into his
mother's soft fur
and went to sleep
soundly in their
cozy den in the snow.